Copyright

All rights reserved.

The characters and events portrayed in this book are fictitious. Any similarity to real persons, living or dead, is coincidental and not intended by the author.

No part of this book may be reproduced, or stored in a retrieval system, or transmitted in any form or by any means, electronic, mechanical, photocopying, recording, or otherwise, without express written permission of the publisher.

ISBN-13: 9781005911225

Contents

Journey to Zoo

Rahul and his family are going to Jurassic zoo but Jurassic zoo is in lord land and Rahul and his family lived in a village will they be able to reach the zoo that we will see in the story.

Chapter 1

Rahul was nine years old his mother decided to go to Jurassic zoo his father took a bus.

Rahul and his family sat on the bus then they had their lunch.

After one-hour Rahul ate an apple at night they slept for eight hours.

Next morning it was a clear day then they saw five peacocks they were dancing it was a sunny day.

They drank some water then the bus reached the zoo.

They took three tickets they entered the Jurassic zoo they had some Food. It was night they slept.

In the morning it was a cool day Rahul, and his family was very happy.

Then they walked to see some animals.

First, they took a photo of an elephant he was taking bath then a baby elephant come running.

He was 1-year old.

Rahul and his family loved him.

Then they walked, to see more animals.

Then they saw a bear he was eating honey.

Then bear started playing with his kids. The kids were sitting on the bear's lap they took a photo of the bear.

Then the kids sat on the bears back.

Rahul and his family were very happy seeing this all.

Then they had their lunch and at night they slept. Next morning, they left for the lord land.

Then they saw a hippo he was swimming.

Rahul and his family saw it then they walked to see some more animals then they saw a tiger he was sleeping in his den.

Rahul and his family saw it then they had their lunch and at night Rahul and his family slept.

Next morning, they walked to see more animals.

They saw a rhinoceros he was eating grass then they drank some water and went to see some more animals.

Then they saw a lion he was siting.

Rahul and his family saw it then they slept.

Next morning it was a sunny day Rahul and his family gone to see some more animals.

Then they saw a crocodile he was walking Rahul and his family had their lunch then they had some juice it was mango juice.

Rahul and his family loved the juice and then they gone to see some more animals then they saw a deer he was running Rahul and his family saw it.

Family looked at him then they had their lunch.

Then Rahul mother decided to go back home.

His father took a bus then Rahul and his sat on the bus.

Then Rahul and his family had their lunch and at night Rahul and his family slept for nine hours next morning.

Rahul and his family walk up they had their breakfast after two days the bus reach to the stop.

Rahul and his family reached home.

Then Rahul and his family had their lunch and told everyone about lord land.

Everyone was happy to listen the story of lord land and everyone gone to lord land.

Lord land became famous and hit.

Maya's Picnic

Maya had a picnic to museum from school, but the bus is scheduled to start at 9 am. Will she be able to reach the museum on time? That we will see in the story.

Chapter 1

Maya has a picnic to museum, so her mother gives her some food.

Then, Maya sat on the bus. The bus started to the picnic place then Maya had her lunch.

then she sang a song. Everyone also sang with Maya.

After 10 hours it was night Maya, and everyone slept for 9 hours.

Then Maya's friend Rohit said to Maya let's play something till our lunch time.

Next morning everyone walks up to Maya. They had her breakfast.

Maya said – "OK, Rohit let's play till the lunch time" After 2 hours it was lunch time.

Maya's Mam told it is lunch time, Kids have you lunch. Everyone had their lunch.

Then after 5 hours it was night everyone slept.

Next morning after 3 hours Rohit said to Maya.

Let's have our lunch from 3 hours, we had nothing Maya said "OK, Rohit".

Then everyone had their lunch after 5 hours it was night everyone slept. Next morning the bus reached to the museum.

Maya come down from the bus she entered the museum then she saw a painting. In the painting she saw many flowers she loved the painting.

Then she saw some portraits. She was very happy seeing this all then she saw architecture. Maya loved that she bought some paintings also. Then Maya sat in the bus to go home. The bus started going.

Then it was night everyone slept after 9 hours.

Maya reached home she come down from the bus and told their mother and father about the museum and showed the paintings that she bought.

From the museum her mother and father where very happy seeing this all.

The Hungry Bear

Chapter 1

Ones upon a time there lived a bear. He was very hungry he didn't eat anything since morning.

He saw a monkey coming, the bear asked, do you have something to eat.

Monkey said "Yes, let's have it together as I have more than I can eat".

Suddenly they saw an elephant coming he said, "Hello can I also have some food". They said yes you can have.

Then they started eating after 20 minutes they thanked the monkey and after that day monkey bear and elephant become very good friends and lived happily thereafter.

Mother's Day

Chapter 1

It is Mother's Day, Johnny is making a cake for his mother it was chocolate cake his mother is 33 years old, so he took two candles from the shop.

Then he invited his friends because he needs help to make a cake for his mother.

Then his friends come to help him then everyone started making the cake then after 30 minutes the cake was ready.

Then everyone putted some balloons then journey decided to surprise his mother then he took the candles in the cake and took the cake on the room.

Then he told his friends to close his mother's eyes and take his mother to the room where the cake and balloons are. His friends did as he told.

Then they took Johnny's mother to the room and said now open your eyes. Johnny's mother opened her eyes and then she saw many balloons.

She felt wonderful. Then she said let us now cut the cake.

Her mother cut the cake, blew the candles, and ate the cake Johnny's mother was very happy and said this is my best day.

The Wedding Party

Chapter 1

Johnny, Pinkie, Rita and Maya are going to a party. They will dance in the stage.

Alex is the Director of the party. He invited everyone.

Johnny was 19 years old; Rita was 15 years old; Alex was 22 years old; Maya was 18 years old and Pinkie was 20 years old. They were going to a party.

Frist Alex putted some balloons then he made some juice then Maya, Rita, Johnny, and Pinkie come to the party.

Alex gave them some juice they drank some juice it was mango juice they loved it.

Then they danced for 1 hour.

Then they drank some water and thanked Alex for the party Alex said always welcome

Then they sat on the bus and went home. After reaching home they told their mother about the party.

Their mother was very happy.

Then their mother made a cake for them, everyone ate the cake and they enjoyed it.

Birthday of Mini

Chapter 1

It is Mini's birthday; her mother is making a cake for her.

Mini is inviting her friend Rohit and Sanvi in the birthday party.

She decorated some balloons, after some time Mini's friend Rohit and Sanvi came to the birthday party.

Then they drank some water and the party started music started everyone danced a lot.

After 30 minutes they drank some water and then they played with balloons.

After 1 hour they decided to go home.

They thanked mini for inviting them to the birthday and went home.

When they reach home, they told their mother and father about the party.

Their mother and father where surprised about their kid's party.

Lori and Nani

Chapter 1

Ones upon a time there lived a cat named Lori, she had a friend named Nani.

Whenever Nani makes food she used to sing –

"Come-come Luri... and eat some food."

Luri comes and eats the food. Nani had a son he thinks why Nani gives more food to lure and gives me less.

He thought let me trouble Luri so she will never come here again.

After 10 days it was Luri's birthday, Nani's son thought let me trouble Luri now.

Nani made some food for Luri and said, "I am going to take a bath and after that everyone will have some food".

Nani son thought let me trouble Lure now he sang in Nani's voice.

"Come-come Luri… and eat some food."

Luri tried to eat the food but the food was hot.

She couldn't eat the food she ran away.

Chapter 2

Then Nani came and said let's have our food let me call lure she sang

"Come-come Lure… and have some food.

Lure didn't come. Nani went to her den and she saw Lure was packing her bag.

She said, "What happen". Lure said now I will never come here. I am going some were else. Nani said, "What happen …. What happen".

Lure said your son gave me hot food.
Nani understood what happen then she
scolded her son. Her son said I don't like
her that's why I trouble her.

Nani told him that ok but don't do this
thing because of your mistake my Lure
has gone and now she will never come
back here.

Nani's son said ok now I will never do
this again. Then Nani went to her room.

Nani son also went to his room and Lure
went some were else.

The Three Birds

Chapter 1

Ones upon a time in a jungle there lived three birds. The first bird's name was Mini, the second bird's name was Mono, and the third bird's name was Lone.

Lone was a small bird he lived with his
mother Mini and his father Mono.

Mono was very hungry, Mini made some
food. Mono went to eat it. Mini said no-
no-no don't eat it now.

I am going to take a bath and then I will give everyone. Mono said ok.

Mini went to take bath. Mono thought mini is not seeing anything.

Let me give Lone a video game and then he went near the food.

He opened the cocker voice came Lone came running and said no don't eat that mom said after 1 hour we will eat. Mono said I am not eating.

Your mom didn't close the cocker, so I am closing.

Lone said "OK, after closing you come" and went to play video game again.

Chapter 2

Mono opened the cocker.

After opening the cocker, he tasted the food it was very nice.

After 12 minutes, Mini came she opened the cocker she saw the food was less.

She asked Mono did you eat some food. Mono said, "No-no I didn't eat".

Then she saw from the other side also it was less then mini knew that Mono has only eaten.

Then Lone said Yes-yes father only ate I saw father opening the cocker mini said let us play in the park who falls in the river he only ate the food.

Everyone went to the park to swing in the park. Mono said First mini will swing.

He thought if mini falls my chance will not come.

Chapter 3

Mini said if I have eaten some food then I fall. Mini swing, but she didn't fall. Mono said no spin fast.

Mono swung it fast but Mini didn't fall then Mini said "Mono it is your turn. Mono said no it is Lone.

Mini said "OK".

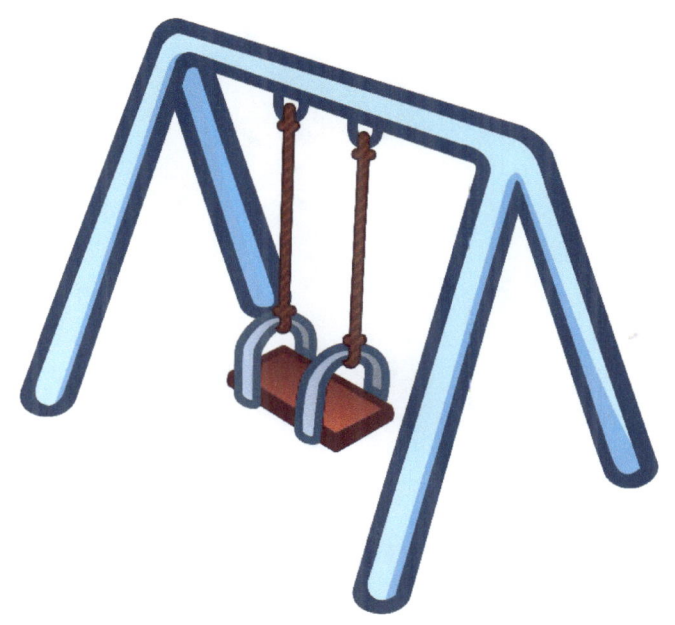

Lone sat on the swing he swigged and said if I have eaten some food, then I fall.

Then he also didn't fall. Then mono said no you swing fast.

Mono swung fast then also Lone didn't fall. Then mini said now Mono it is your turn.

Mono sat in the swing and said if I have eaten some food then I fall.

Mono fell in the river he said Yes, I have eaten some food but help me now Mini said OK.

Mini and Lone took Mono out of the river and celebrated the birthday of Lone.

Lone ate some food mini also ate some food.

Then lone played with balloons

and had his lunch and talked to his mother and father Thanking them for setting his birthday party and played with his friends and told them about his birthday party.

His friends loved his birthday party and they also celebrated their birthday party, the way Lone celebrated.

The Bird and the Mouse

Chapter 1

Once upon a time there lived a bird named Mini.

She had 3 children.

Every day she goes to search some food for her children from the farm.

One day the farmer wondered where my food is going away every day.

He got an idea. He kept a net. When the bird came, she got trapped.

She couldn't go and give her children food.
Because her legs were stuck in the net.

the farmer took her with him to his house in the village.

She sang - "Do you know that near the Lake there are my kids.

in my house Tam Rak Too...!!"

They are waiting for me to come Tam
Rak Too...

She was telling many times, but he did
not listen.
The farmer thought she is telling lies so
that I leave her. The farmer didn't let her
go.

Then it was evening the kids were
waiting for Mother to come.

They didn't have eaten any food since morning. They were very hungry.

Chapter 2

Suddenly she saw a mouse coming she thought this mouse can help me.

She sang again – "Do you know that near the lake there are my kids Tam Rak Too...!!"

"My kids are waiting for me to come Tam Rak Too...!!"

The mouse thought let me help her.

He saw the farmer sleeping.

Mouse broke the net. The bird came out and thanked the mouse. She took some food from the farm and gave to her children.

Then one day a flood came the mouse fell in the water he shouted.

"Help me - Help me."

The bird saw the mouse she said that mouse only helped me I should also help him.

She flew over the water and pulled mouse out from the lake.

Thank You!!!

The mouse thanked the bird.

The bird said you helped me, and I helped you so no THANK YOU.

After that, the mouse and the bird became very good friends and lived happily ever after...!!

The End

About the Author

Vihan Telang is an eight-year-old kid from Hyderabad, India. He is very much inspired by re-known Children book author Ruskin Bond. In the book "Journey to Zoo", Vihan has narrated about some of his experiences from his recent visit to Chester Zoo near Liverpool, UK. His favorite book is "Getting Granny's Glasses" by Ruskin Bond. He is a 3rd grade student and his favorite subject is Mathematics. Other than writing he enjoys dancing, singing, doing art and craft. He is also working on his second story book titled - "Story of Two Puppets".